Rainbow People

Nicholas Mosley

RAINBOW PEOPLE

A SEQUEL TO *METAMORPHOSIS*

AND *TUNNEL OF BABEL*

First Dalkey Archive edition, 2018.

Library of Congress Cataloging-in-Publication Data
Names: Mosley, Nicholas, 1923-2017, author.
Title: Rainbow people / by Nicholas Mosley.
Description: First Dalkey Archive edition. | Victoria, TX : Dalkey Archive Press, 2018. | "A sequel to Metamorphosis and Tunnel of Babel."
Identifiers: LCCN 2017057597 | ISBN 9781628972283 (pbk. : alk. paper)
Classification: LCC PR6063.O82 R35 2018 | DDC 823/.914--dc23
LC record available at https://lccn.loc.gov/2017057597

www.dalkeyarchive.com
Victoria, TX / McLean, IL / Dublin

Dalkey Archive Press publications are, in part, made possible through the support of the University of Houston-Victoria and its programs in creative writing, publishing, and translation.

Printed on permanent/durable acid-free paper.

INTRODUCTION

In the middle years of the previous century the philosopher Karl Jaspers wrote about the major changes in human consciousness which seemed to have occurred around halfway through the last millennium BC – the age of the Old Testament prophets which led on to the following centuries of the Greek Philosophers and Dramatists. This was an age when human beings felt themselves able to challenge their natural instincts and attitudes by systems of faith or reason. Jaspers also remarked that it seemed to him there were signs of a possibly similar change approaching the start of the third millennium AD. He gave few instances of what these might be. Jaspers died in 1969. Since then the most notable that has come to the attention of educationists and social workers (though not to scientists or philosophers) is the emergence of a category labelled as Rainbow Children. – This term has been coined to represent a species of children who are different enough to make them distinct from normality by virtue of the intensity of their curiosity for how things worked, or should work, in the world around them, combined with a gentleness and even 'sweetness' of disposition to others. The word 'rainbow', used as an adjective, evolved from preliminary efforts at categorising children as 'Indigo' or 'Crystal', though it was never claimed that such terms were gained scientifically. Nor was it yet being suggested that such ideas were applicable to all humans rather than just children. There is also not much talk about how adults should deal with such children.

It seemed to me, however, the author of this sequel, that if the word 'Rainbow' was to mean anything, at least in their way of looking at it, it should be considered worth investigating by grown-ups.

What concentrated my interest were the accounts of large bands of refugees moving from the Middle East or Africa into Europe, and the extraordinary stories of the careful and deliberate plans made by these people before they set off on their journeys. These stories emphasised the way such bands of so-called fugitives organised themselves before they set off, by ensuring that they would have enough money and provisions to enable them to reach at least the first frontier at which they would be forced to stop or pause. And when this happened, it did not seem they were disconcerted or forced to turn back; they felt it necessary to wait where they were, and where they had foreseen the possibility of having to support themselves, until it became clear what options might be available to them. They apparently did not, for instance, consider hiring boats or boatmen to take them across the Aegean Sea, but rather insisted on making sure that such boats were in their possession so they could have some confidence in not being betrayed.

From this situation, public reports seem to tell either of accidental disaster such as overloaded boats sinking and hundreds being drowned; or, mysteriously the success of their undertaking by news of their acceptance in a new home such as Austria or Germany. By this time a suitable word to describe these people who made it stopped being 'refugees' or 'fugitives', but rather 'immigrants' or 'settlers'. It seemed to be in no one's interest to describe their stories in detail because the chance of them evolving as hoped for depended on them being protected from the hostility of others, and old-fashioned opposing forces. The success of new forces depended on the confidence and assurance of something that should not be made vulnerable in words. Except perhaps a word denoting hope, that it was up to one to make what one likes of such a situation by a word such as 'Rainbow'. Of course, these people would not be restricted to their being immigrants or children, although such words would be as distinctive as 'Rainbow' – a mysterious-seeming occurrence formed by sunlight passing through raindrops and appearing as if magically like a bridge between one state of existence, that of refugees, and another, that of immigrants.

Rainbow People

1.

A YOUNG WOMAN AND a young man are walking along a sandy path above a coastline, with a young child walking between them. They appear to be having a conversation with one another over the head of the child, although sometimes it also seems that they may be intending to impart information to the child. The child sometimes looks up at one or the other of them, before returning to what seems to be his major interest, which is kicking with his feet any stones that are in his path.

The young man was saying, 'We are going to watch a film being made – you know, a film such as we sometimes see on the television. This film is special to your mother and me because we made friends with the director, who is in charge of what the film is trying to say.' The young woman says, 'Your father had a hand in writing the scene we are going to see.' 'Though goodness knows what they'll make of it,' the young man says. The child smiles.

After a few paces, the young man continues, 'They are leaving the country in which they have been brought up because the conditions there have become intolerable for them. So in a sense they are fleeing from these conditions, but at the same time they are hoping, and intending, to find a new location that will be better for them, and they might even be the better for it. But, of course, amongst the people they have left behind there are many who will feel they are traitors or deserters; and amongst the people in the countries to which they are heading, many will see them as interlopers and thus enemies. And indeed, it is in these guises that the rest of the world sees them, as people who will, each way, disturb the status quo.'

The young woman says, as if interrupting, 'This is the way human beings seem to like to see things. As states of affairs, or persons, who are naturally either friends or enemies, rather than being creatures who can be gentle, or according to plan, turned from one to the other.'

The child had picked up a stone from the path, and seemed to be about to throw it into the bushes, when he held it again carefully under his face, then placed it carefully in the grass at the side of the road. The man and the woman had stopped, and watched him. The man said quietly, 'You think he understands.' The woman said, 'I don't know about the words.' The child stands a few paces ahead with his back to them. He then runs forward at a pace that they had not seen him manage before. He comes to where the path splits into two, one going straight along beside where there is now visible an inlet from the sea, the other making a sharp right turn as if following the requirements of the sea. The child has stopped running. He looks down towards whatever may be on his right. Then he slowly and, as if deliberately, falls flat on his face.

The young man, his father, gives a jump, then puts his hand dramatically against where there might be his heart.

He says, 'It's the uncertainty.'

The woman says, 'That matters.'

'That lets you make up your mind?'

'Or your heart.'

They began to walk side by side to where the child had fallen. By the time they reached him he had sat up, and was looking down to his right to where the sea must be. The man and woman could see what he was watching, which was a wide sandy beach at the end of the inlet from the sea.

On the beach, there was a boat on the sand, and in the shallow water there was a group of men and women, mostly young, who were in swimsuits or their underwear playing some game with a ball or else simply frolicking. The man and woman stood by the child and watched. The man said, 'That's the film crew?' The woman said, 'That's reality.' The man said, as if to the boy, 'They're resting.' Then he looked back at the scene on the beach below. He said, 'Nicely, violently.'

The woman said, as if to the child, 'They're the actors.' The child said quietly, 'I like them.'

At the far side of the bay, on a rocky and grass-covered headland which projected into the sea, the further rocky headland from the one on which the man and woman and child were standing, there was a group of people who seemed to be unmistakably technicians and directing staff of a film crew. There were two cameras on trolleys, audio equipment, and a man standing holding a megaphone, looking down at the people gambolling on the beach. When he noticed the man, woman, and child on the opposite headland he raised his megaphone to his mouth and shouted, 'Action in fifteen minutes.' The people on the beach seemed to pay no attention to him. One of the men standing by a camera swivelled it round and directed it onto the people on the beach. After a minute or so the people who were playing seemed to realise they were being filmed and stopped their antics, then walked slowly and, as if reluctantly, to a group of rocks at the back of the beach where there appeared to be some discarded clothes lying. They began slowly to put these on. The clothes were overtly reminiscent of those worn by refugees, as seen and photographed in the newspapers. On the higher ground behind them the man with the megaphone shouted, 'Stop that!' And the man who had been working the camera stepped back from it, having apparently switched it off. The people who had been having fun on the watersedge continued slowly putting on the clothes taken up from the rocks; these were mostly unkempt and sometimes patched up garments that people in poverty in the Middle East might be wearing. When they had done this they stood around as if in a depressed state; as if they were in fact acting. Everything seemed to have come to a halt. The young man said quietly to the young woman, 'This is no good.' The young woman said, 'Yes. It depends on what happens next.' The child, who had been watching the scene on the beach, looked up at his father, then wandered off along the path on which they had been travelling. Then the child left the path, as if absentmindedly, and scrambled cautiously towards the sea. He was now some distance from the beach. He broke into a stumbling run down the rocks, and then without warning seemed to jump, or flop, into the sea. He managed somehow to get quite a distance from both the rocks and the sandy beach, and then, as if he might have lost his nerve or perhaps been attacked from under the surface, he appeared suddenly to be in great difficulties, as if he might drown. The young man, when the child had moved away from its mother and himself, had shouted 'Oi.'

Now he began to run, and scrambled recklessly over the rocks towards the sea. The young woman stayed where she was and said, not very loudly, 'No.' The man seemed to hear her and stopped at the edge of the rocks, sat down and watched where the child appeared to be in difficulties in the water. The woman, who was some way back from all this, said quietly, 'I have taught him how to swim.' The man said nothing. On the opposite side of the bay, the man who had been in charge of one of the cameras had swivelled it around, as if to film where the child was in the water. And the young man and woman did not do anything. The man, the child's father, was thinking, You mean they might, they should, be filming this? He lay back on the rocks as though he were very tired. On the beach the people who had been dressing themselves in their rough clothes as actors began rapidly to tear them off, and then dashed back into the sea. The camera man swivelled the camera again to include the young man and young woman on the far promontory. He spent some time adjusting the camera so that it could take in the whole scene, with the child in the centre of it. Then he stood back, as if to be able to see what was happening with his own eyes. On the promontory behind him, the man with the megaphone, who had just previously shouted 'Stop that', now put it to his mouth again and yelled 'Action!' The child, who had appeared – for a stroke or two – to have been swimming, now suddenly, and as if acting, raised his arms and sank beneath the surface. On the rocks somewhere behind him, his mother, the young woman said, 'I taught him just the other day. I should have told you.' The young man said nothing. The man who had been in charge of the camera now moved away from it and sat on the sandy beach just short of the water line as if he might be exhausted. The group of people who had taken off their actors' clothes to dash to the water, plunged into the sea in the direction of the child. Leading them were four young people who were almost naked.

The young man now sat down and held his head in his hands. It was if he was hearing a voice in his head saying – You mean cameras can make things clearer? And then the answering voice of himself – If it is put up against reality. The four young men and women reached the child who had succeeded in appearing to drown, but also expertly to have kept afloat. One of the men said, 'Put him on my back.' One of the women answered, 'No, I've got him.' The three of them began to swim confidently towards the shore and then wade back to the beach. The child was smiling. The young woman on the promontory, its mother, seemed to be kneeling with her head almost banging on the rocks in front of her. The child reached the sandy beach, crawled and then stood and waved to its mother. After a moment she looked up and waved back with both arms. The young man, who was the child's father, had a voice in his head saying to himself – When did you teach him to swim. The young woman was saying in his head – I can't remember.

The man with the megaphone on the opposite headland shouted, 'We got that, right?' The group who had torn off their actors' clothes to help the child, now formed a circle around the smiling child on the beach, as if they were in some way honouring him. There did not seem to be anyone filming this. The young man and woman on the opposite promontory stood on the path side by side, like statues, watching. The young woman, who was called Jenny, was thinking, Of course, humans think that one thing happens after another that causes it, but in what might be called reality everything happens all at once.

The man and woman who had been the first to reach the child when it was in the water were remembering – or the man was remembering – it's all right I've got him. The woman was trying to remember – was he or was he not drowning? But does this matter? Then carrying on now while they were sitting in the circle, the others who had thrown themselves into trying to rescue the child were thinking – both yes and no, it does and doesn't matter. The man who had been with her was thinking – if it is what happens that matters, then that is all right. The woman called Jenny, standing on the rocks, said, 'I can't remember when l taught him.' It was then that the man with the megaphone on the opposite headland called 'Action!' again. The young man with Jenny, who was called Richard, said, 'Anyway, that might do it.' The child, who was at the centre of the circle, now looked at its mother and father and waved. Richard and Jenny, after a moment, waved back.

Then Richard said quietly, 'Do you think he knew what would happen?' Jenny said, 'I don't know. He knew what was happening.' Richard said, 'He couldn't have planned it.'Jenny said, 'No.'Richard said, 'You think it comes as a sort of vision: an impulse?'Jenny said, 'Yes, but those are words.'Richard said, 'And then what happens.'

On the beach the circle of people around the child were gazing at him as if he were imparting something to them. The man with the megaphone, who was called Cyril, had come down from the rocks on the far side of the beach and was crossing the sand towards where Jenny and Richard were now sitting, as if to wait more patiently. Richard, watching him, murmured,

'How much does he know?' Jenny said, 'We had that long talk with him in Geneva. He's been watching now what happens.' Richard said, 'What did he say then. What will he do now?'

Jenny said, 'When the refugees set off they are not like fugitives. They usually have enough money and food with them to see them through to the first critical frontier on their planned journey. This is, of course, sometimes, if not all that often, insufficient. And the press reporters who will be watching out for this will make the best of it, the stories of hunger and extreme distress that keep their readers, and thus themselves, happy.'

Richard said 'And then what.'

By this time, the man called Cyril had reached where they were sitting. Jenny murmured something, and the man held out his hand to Richard, who took it. Cyril then sat down on the far side of Jenny. Jenny was saying, 'You have to keep this secret.' Richard said, 'Local people will try to stop it because they have become accustomed to all this, and if the refugees were encouraged to stay, they worry how that might be bad for them.' Cyril chipped in, 'That is not difficult to understand, what is difficult is to try to tell the truth. At least in matters of social urgency.'

On the beach the group around the child was slowly breaking up. Cyril said, 'They do not turn back. That is not their nature. On the borders of Greece and Macedonia, which is here, there are literally thousands of people who have great camps of wooden huts or tents, often with the political and financial help of charitable groups like Oxfam, but also with the aid of local people. When these people have seen the refugees' steadfastness and friendliness, they are impelled, they may not know why, to help them, especially so-called refugees who have managed to bring enough money, as well as a climate of hope and faith, which local people recognise, and find that they wish to assist them. The strangeness of this situation could alter, or even completely change, what might have become ordinary social behaviour. It is the anomaly in all this that may seem to the outside world to be double-think or secrecy – either way. There is not much for the press to say about any of it.

'The duplicity or maybe truthfulness – whatever it is, it seems to be in no one's interest to know. It also seems not to be in the interest of those in power to talk about it; certainly not in the countries which the fugitives are aiming for. But one of the qualities of being in power involves a sort of recognition of what might be truthfulness, and at the same time the need, if this is to work itself out, of secrecy. Because any sort of solution in words would prevent things working themselves out naturally. And thus would not even be profitable. But with people in authority, there might still be some sort of understanding, because their business demands secrecy. Such are the rules of the game of power, and why not in the larger spectacle of outcome. This is why there seems to be a strange, unspoken grace or sensibility amongst those in authority in the countries which the refugees choose!'

Jenny suddenly shouted and waved, as if in the direction in which the child had been sitting with his audience around him. The child, who was now on her lap, smiled and looked up at her. Cyril said, 'Yes, eventually.' Richard was thinking – but he's already here on her lap. It seemed that on the far promontory there were people still filming. But was not everything quiet. Nothing much, at least here, was actively happening. On their rocky promontory, Cyril was saying, 'You think he might even be informing them of what may be coming.' Jenny said, 'Well, we need provisions, whatever may be not happening.' After a pause, Richard said, 'This is far deeper than a film.' Then Richard lay back as if waiting for sleep to come.

After a time, Cyril said, 'This is what I have learned, or perhaps my imagination has run away with me, since I was last talking with you in Geneva. That in the public or official eye, there is, owing to the disturbance, what may look like some Civil War in the Middle East. Certain denizens have taken the step of not only leaving their homeland but also their customs of mind; that is, "to have a go" necessitates a *both* and not an *either/or*. "To have a go" means it's the most one can do to succeed in this; to "have a go" is the best one can do. Even if indistinctly, in one's mind. To "have a go" seems to include making preparations but not – if one is not to go the wrong way – to make more than imaginary plans. The reason for this seems to be – as may become more apparent according to what the situation requires – that the story of a success may become more apparent than the story of a withdrawal, so long as no one has the temerity to suggest otherwise. For, although it may seem customary for people in trouble to be helped, for them to be successful seems largely out of their hands. And so people who have been categorised as fugitives suddenly become those heading over a rainbow to a new existence – to one that is of a new nature – one which is reached by the recognition that sunlight and raindrops need not be opposites, but can together make something beautiful and the same. It may still be that efforts to success bring them sympathy, rather than suffering the result of failure. But with luck, the new arrivals may settle down to work together with the people around them, who will welcome them. Has there not always been something of this when new arrivals, such as colonials, come into a country that has begun to experience stagnation rather than peace. This may be described in the phase of the conversion of raindrops and sunlight. The danger had been that inhabitants and new arrivals could find themselves relaxing; unless they have experiences even in small things they may not be able to find peace; unless, as it were, they see it in the terms that gave them opportunity, that of the rainbow. This way of looking at the state of affairs, resulting from their journey, demands to be sustained in mind and imagination. The way this might happen is by recognition of the existence of the rainbow, rainbows, in their heads. If they do this, people around them, even if they do not see clearly, can realise that humans do not see the sunlight and raindrops in the rainbow, but they can see what it is that *exists*. That is, huts and tents on the frontier, all the rewards of charity, or the style of people remember this when they are able to settle down and work to change the world. Or to keep the world the same. What's the difference.'

*

All this system, of either ignorance or deception, was of course nothing strange to the people who were officiating and in charge of what was going on at frontiers. There were people who were responsible for passing on orders from the politicians to the frontier police and they would, as a result of the nature of the job, get quite used to being involved with orders that they either suspected or knew to be double-dealing or duplicitous. Whatever state of mind that is. Throughout the ages people have managed to discover through exploration. This may be enhanced by risk, hardship, and apparent danger, because these feed the human love of the exotic and exciting, whatever difficulty these experiences bring with them, being part of and not detrimental to them, and the feeling that is in this that life becomes worth living.

The three people, Jenny Richard and Cyril, sitting on the rocks on the far side of the beach from the filmmakers, had been watching what was going on on the sand of the bay, where the child had been surrounded by those who had seemed to be trying to hear him speak. But surely he had been saying nothing. On the promontory at the far side of the bay the film crew were moving restlessly, as though waiting for something further to happen. Cyril looked up and seemed to be hoping to find something as well. It was if there was a vacancy in communication and orders.

Then Cyril continued, 'All this system of either ignorance or deception was of course nothing strange to the people who were officially in charge of what was going on at the frontier. They were the people responsible for passing on orders to armed police at the frontier – presumably about who should be let through, or not. But now nothing like this seemed to be happening so what might they be expected to do – work things out on their own initiative?' A thought came into Richard's head – or perhaps they were just hungry. But how could the refugees in this situation take any initiative?

The actors on the beach seemed to be restlessly looking up at the track which went from where they had set up their cameras inland to the village Richard remembered from a conversation he had overheard, at least in his mind, between Cyril and the woman that they knew to be his wife. Cyril had been telling her to hurry back to the village and tell the providers of sustenance to cancel such an order. Could this be possible? He had heard Cyril giving some sort of explanation to one of his colleagues, which was that he required his actors to be hungry so they would better represent the situation of the refugees they were acting. But also, had this happened or was it part of a story picturing futility? Or might this be a necessary impetus to action? And so what could they do but wait to see what would happen – the frontier officials restless, as if they had learned no confidence in waiting. But how should Richard know whether what he thought he had heard was what would happen. That is to see what would happen next. It was true, of course, that their orders were sometimes to let a considerable group of refugees through. But their job seemed to demand that nothing should be openly questioned, or the trouble that might depend on those in authority could well depend on them. There came into Jenny's head, Humans have up till now imagined that it is their duty to find answers to problematic situations which face them, but what I have learned is that it is unlikely that one will find helpful solutions this way. What one has to do is wait and watch what is happening, so that they see the things that are required from them. Jenny was thinking, On the frontier, for instance, between Greece and Macedonia, which is where we might be now, except that we had to choose somewhere different, out of the ordinary, so we could film it without interruptions, but of course there are interruptions. But goodness knows, one can see that it is the laws which have been made by distant but opportunistic others, who might otherwise see, from what is in front of their eyes, the sense of letting many people through the frontier at intervals during each week; it is likely that they will have had contact with the people on the other side guarding the frontier, who might have intimated that it could profit them too if people were let through. These people might do work that was selected for them that local people were too hidebound to do themselves, as long as things weren't talked about in such terms of personal responsibility. Jenny said 'Of course it is not easy to film here something that is so secret, if it is to work smoothly.'

Cyril said, 'Yes, it is not possible to foretell. There will be something happening or not happening here, and we are waiting.'

Richard said, 'Yes, we all are as a matter of fact getting hungry.'

Jenny said to Cyril, 'When did your people last eat?'

Cyril said, 'Yesterday evening. I wanted them to experience what it can feel like to be hungry.'

Jenny said, 'So you told your wife to get back to the village quickly and stop the truck arriving.'

Richard said, 'But that's ridiculous.'

Jenny said, 'But what we are saying is, indeed, that all this is ridiculous.'

Richard said, 'But, whatever may happen here, it will not be equivalent to what is happening on the border of Greece and Macedonia.'

Cyril said, 'Well, things both here and there

people may begin to see as being ridiculous.'

Richard said, 'But can you say hunger is ridiculous.'

'If it is unnecessary, yes.'

Jenny said, 'And that may be a way to learn.'

Richard said, 'And you think the world might change if people realised how ridiculous they are.'

Jenny said, 'Even now, we seem to have learnt something of how ridiculous war is. But we are imbued with the idea that something should be done rapidly about a situation in which we find ourselves. And so we bomb people who we think must be causing the troubles, here or there, people in authority or subordinate, who it seems easy for us to say are causing the trouble, when in fact we don't know who they are. They are just given initials, which hardly helps them to learn for themselves what they are, and nowadays there seems to be no requirement to learn what the effects of bombs are. The usefulness of news which reports random bombing is to learn to see things like this, but then surely such a state of affairs is ridiculous.'

After a pause, Jenny said, 'And you think people may learn this?'

Richard said, 'What else is the point of films?'

Richard continued, 'And so we need laughter.'

Jenny said, 'And tenderness. That is the point of the child.'

Richard said, 'By the way, where is the child?'

Cyril said, 'Can one say, going about his business? And all the wonderful Oxfam extras who no one knows exactly who they are.'

Richard said, 'And so secretly this is a time of peace.'

Jenny said, 'But how does a situation of peace and tenderness come about if people have always seen war as a way of demonstrating the sincerity of their obsessions.'

Cyril said, 'You may be vulnerable. How do you prevent that?'

Jenny said, 'You just do.'

After a pause, Cyril said, 'And there is the larger oddity of what is happening on the ground. There seems to be, and is, war in the Middle East, but not war in the old sense of knowing one's enemy, choosing one's enemy, and being able to try and win on the ground. Now there is chaos. Who is whose enemy seems to happen by chance, and yet one still has the impression this should and can be stopped by war. That is, by sending in bombers and dropping bombs, one may not know exactly where. But that is the point. Do you know the history of the so-called war in Mesopotamia in the early 1920s, after the end of the first so-called World War? This Mesopotamian War is said to have been won by the head of the RAF at that time, someone called John Salmond. He had no troops to give orders to on the ground, but the random, and yet not in the event random, bombing had the effect of making them want to stop the violence on the ground, because there seemed to be no sense in war anymore, and perhaps never had been. Anyway, the war in Mesopotamia ended with people coming together at a place, the name of which I cannot even now remember, and agreeing that what was being learned was not who the winners were and who the losers were. One's duty as families on the ground was just to learn how to stay alive while the rest of the world might go mad.' Richard said, 'Yes, my mother Johanna used to know that RAF man.' Cyril said, 'And I heard on the news that nowadays all Germans are being instructed not to think about who might be enemies, but to lay in stores to ensure that they would be able to survive in conditions of chaos.' And Jenny said, 'Yes, and have you ever had the experience, l mean you yourselves, of when you are looking at a blank wall, and you stop trying to focus, because it is tiring your eyes, and there comes into your vision, on the previously blank wall, an extraordinary tapestry or frieze of innumerable objects, animal, vegetable, and mineral? I It makes it easy to accept, almost be overwhelmed by, a work of art with no meaning except that, of course, of a work in which beauty and strangeness have meaning.'

Cyril said, 'Yes, I see that.'

Richard said, 'When we look at frontiers we see not only a blank wall with no answers but also, if we admit our eyes are tired, we see a world that depends on us, and only if we allow it to exercise its own meaning.' After a long silence, Richard continued, 'So are the Germans obeying the advice of their government?' Cyril said, 'That is a question to which there are no answers as long as it is questioned.'

On the opposite promontory from where they were sitting some activity was going on, with people's attention being drawn to something happening on the track from the village to where the film crew had set themselves up. People seemed to be waving at something out of sight along this track. Either to encourage it or discourage it to come on or not. The child, who had been on Jenny's lap, had climbed off it while Jenny was talking, as if he were fed up.

He ran or clambered over the rocks and sand of the bay until he could be in a position to see what was happening further down the track. Cyril was saying, 'That will be the van of provisions arriving from the village.' Richard said, 'I thought you had cancelled that in order to keep your actors hungry?' Cyril said, 'Yes, but then I cancelled that cancellation.' Jenny said, 'Which you couldn't have done if you hadn't said it.' Richard said, 'But you can film the outcome of it.' Cyril said, 'I hope so.' He stood up and began to walk slowly along the beach to where the child was standing. Jenny said, as if to someone just in front of her, 'You mean war becomes boring.' Richard said, 'Doesn't stockpiling become boring.' 'Not if you don't think you know who or what it is for.' Richard said, 'Then it becomes what.' Jenny said, 'Trusting.'

Cyril had reached the far side of the beach, and he sat down just below where the child was watching the track that went inland to the village. After a pause there came into sight a van like those used to deliver groceries. In front of it there were people both beckoning it on, as well as those making gestures for it to go back. Richard said, 'But what are you trusting.' Jenny said, 'As I have so often said, "what happens".' Richard said, 'And that doesn't become boring.' Jenny said, 'No. I've told you my stories about seeing tapestries and engravings on the walls..' Richard said, 'Yes, you mean that's the point of art. Beauty. One can't know what is happening.'

Jenny said, 'And one doesn't want to explain what is happening.'

Cyril, on the beach below, stood up and put his megaphone to his mouth. And then lowered it. The child had crawled up the rocks to the edge of the track as if it might be trying to reach the van, then stopped just short of it. Below him Cyril had again put the megaphone to his mouth, and then lowered it. There was an argument going on between the people trying to encourage the van and those trying to prevent it, seeming almost to come to blows.

Then someone who could not be identified, from the beach, must have climbed into the now vacated driving seat of the van and started up the engine. Cyril thought – that might be my wife to whom I quite naturally gave contradictory orders. The van was being driven as if it was trying to turn around in the narrow space of the track, with its nose first going off the track in the far direction and then reversing. Whoever was driving it seemed then to lose concentration, or her foot slipped on the pedal, because the back of the truck now came over the edge of the track, above the beach, as if it might slide down there and crash. And in so doing it would crush the child beneath it. Cyril again put the megaphone to his mouth then realised that the child was no longer there. He lowered his megaphone; and, as he feared, the back of the van came over the edge of the track with a bump and seemed to be on its way disastrously to the beach. Then the back doors of the van flew open as if through gravity, or like wings opening, and enumerate packets of what might be provisions for individuals tumbled out toward the beach. After these, very slowly, a large barrel or container of liquid appeared from the back of the now almost empty van, and Cyril thought, but if that lands on the rocks they will smash it. He lunged forward as if to put his own body in the way and prevent this; but then a solitary rock on the slope diverted the barrel on its descent and it missed him. Cyril said, as if to himself, from outside himself – 'Thanks.' Then – 'Now, no more questioning.' He turned to the beach where now all the film crew, both actors and technicians, were collecting the seemingly innumerable packages of provisions. The child was being offered a package by one of the crew but was shaking his head. Cyril sat down by the child and said, 'Go on take it. I'll have some of it with you.' On the far side of the beach Richard was saying to Jenny, 'And that's an explanation?' Jenny said, 'No, an encouragement.' Richard said, 'To trust something that one cannot know?' Jenny said, 'No, the way you can learn the unknown by what happens. Or indeed, what is happening.'

At the far side of the bay Cyril was trying to remember his conversation with Jenny and Richard. He had been saying, 'But of course there is free will, but this is activated by what is served up to one. It is like a game, perhaps of tennis. The umpire and linesman are the people who know what are called rules and stick to them. You can serve and then react to what is returned to you. This system is called reality but the functionaries are yourself and whoever or whatever is on the other side of the net. A rally will go on until there is some breakdown. But here it's as if the enemy are the umpire and linesmen, but then the rules order the game to start up again and so it goes on. Richard had said, 'So all right, life is a game.' Jenny had said, 'But there is faith, hope and charity.' Cyril had said, 'Yes, as you so often say, which are seen to live or die according to what happens.' Cyril was now sitting on the beach, with members of his film crew scattered on the sand sleepily around him. The only other human who seemed to be somewhat agitated, certainly lively, was the child, who was standing up and pulling at his swimming pants as if he might need to have a shit or a pee. A thought came into Cyril's head – but we can get rid of waste matter can't we? And then his own voice in his head answered him – But only to make room for more. Jenny's voice was saying to him – Or the game could not go on. Cyril was answering her – No, but then where is it going. A voice came into his head from somewhere or someone he did not know, saying – A game is not going anywhere, it is making stillness a way of expressing reality; like a work of art. Or at least – where the hell does it come from – those things which appear on furniture or empty walls when the eyes are tired of trying to pinpoint particulars, by which they are able to keep out reality. The child, who was a few paces from Cyril, had succeeded in pulling the pants of his swimsuit down and was now managing to pee on the sand in front of him. While this was happening, a figure lay next to him dressed from neck to toes in a long robe with a cowl over its head, with just a narrow slit where its mouth might be. As the child was peeing, a hand appeared mysteriously from the amplitude of the material covering it and seemed to be trying to catch, or at least make contact with, the child's urine. He managed to do this, moved his hand back inside his coverings, and then it appeared again, as if from his neck, exactly above the slit which seemed to be in line with his mouth. Cyril thought – He wants to smell it? Taste it. You can learn from opposites? Then the hand withdrew itself once more under its shroud. In Cyril's head Jenny was saying – You can learn from things when they stop being a game. Richard's voice was saying – And when is that. Jenny's voice was saying – Love, lust, super-symmetry. Richard said – Because they are represented by the illusion of a tapestry on a blank wall. Jenny said – The reality of what is turned by your mind into a game. On the beach it seemed like the child had turned to face Cyril. A voice came from somewhere, 'You mean, you can't talk about it; only experience it.' The child, who was walking towards Cyril, seemed to be saying, 'That's right.' He thought – At least I know now that he is a boy and not a girl, which might be called a reality but seems to be learnt by means of waste matter. Richard's voice then said – But that is reality. Jenny's voice said – It is what you pinpoint by sight, rather than the frieze which envelops everything, which is, if one can describe it, a more real reality.

*

Some days, or was it weeks, later when Richard and Jenny and the child had arrived back in England, Richard was sitting in a deckchair on a lawn and was reading a voluminous Sunday paper. Jenny was teaching the child how to get balls through a hoop. Richard said loudly, 'Look! Here it is.' And then he read, as though it was a quote from the newspaper, 'Austrians and Germans admit accepting into their country tens of thousands, nobody knows how many, so-called refugees.' Jenny said, 'Does it say why they are doing this?' Richard said, 'No, of course it doesn't. You remember my dream.' Jenny said lazily, 'Oh, your dream', 'You know how I said it didn't seem like a dream.' While Jenny was looking away, the child surreptitiously pushed a ball into a more easy position to go into a hoop. Richard put his newspaper down and lay back. He said, 'Theirs was the frontier that we never quite got to. How could we know what it looked like? It was a system of barbed-wire fences more than a person high and stretching – oh I don't know –into infinity. There were men and women in official clothing, you remember their clothing. They were working quietly with instruments like wire cutters on the stands of the fence. Cyril was going up to them and saying quietly, 'What are you doing.' One of the men with wire clippers put a finger to his lips. Cyril turned his back to them. He seemed to beckon to some figures crouching in the dark behind him. They came forward, still crouching, as if that would keep them out of sight. There was a whole stream of them, like a river shimmering in the moonlight. Except there was no moon.' Then, after a pause, 'I see what you mean – yes, but how might anyone worry about numbers, a crowd, a galaxy, signifying – numbers. I told you at the time, I did not think this could be a dream. And now it wasn't.' Richard said, 'Yes, and now it seems it wasn't.' While his mother was thus distracted, the child pushed a croquet ball with his toe through a hoop. Jenny said, 'But you mean, it doesn't matter if it happens – what is called real.'

Richard said, 'Have you heard from Cyril?' Jenny said, 'Yes, things are going well.' Richard said, 'You mean, things are all right if one is given enough information about how things can happen, not how things must happen. If you go for the latter, you find yourself scratching your eyes. Jenny was thinking – and I was dreaming about whether or not she or he was a boy or a girl. And the answer was, well, yes; yes, in so far as nothing is of itself waste matter.

*

'The point of all this is, perhaps' – this is Cyril talking – 'that the rise in respect for uncertainty seems indeed to be having the required, but hardly hoped for, effect. That is –if you do not know who your enemy is then it is difficult to accept the customs of war. Everything becomes a jumble, as when you are looking at something understandable on a wall and it turns into a myriad of interminable and indeterminate effects, if you allow your eyes to do their job without aggression or arrogance. If you cannot draw frontiers, at least one frontier, around an enemy, then what is the point of calling it a war. You are just dropping shells where your own forces seem in not too much danger and then, in this vacancy, there is room for people to see what is to their advantage, so long as it is not exposed to other people's contumely. So, as if for the first time in history, politics seems to be assuming a style of good manners or even – as those who adopted the idea of Rainbow – what they referred to as "sweetness". Thus in Jenny's vision, imagination, or dream, a panoply of affable serenity comes into existence; not at your command but at your invitation. But then – who or what is it that comes in. This is an unnecessary and a solipsistic question; that is, you hold the possibilities in your hands. They either find freedom or they do not. The rainbow comes to you; though you may still recognise it or not.

'The change which Jaspers foretold seems to be to a large extent the way words are used. In the ancient days of Old Testament prophets and Greek philosophers, words were there to be obeyed. In the new dispensation words are there to be hummed or danced to.'

*

At this point in the story of Jenny, Richard, Cyril and the child – most of which was possibly put into book form by Richard – the scene changes; Richard, Jenny and the child have gone back to England. Cyril takes his crew to film several locations and a bit of activity around the Turkish-Greek borders next to the Aegean Sea. Back in England, Richard and Jenny discuss whether to go back to the home that they had set up in the area of Lake Geneva, where the child has made friends in an infant school. Richard said, 'But the setting is changing. The crisis in Geneva when that vast underground monster machine, the large Hadron Collider, was giving the world, in its own strange way, the information that was needed to herald the possible, indeed likely, change in human consciousness, and that would begin to take place at the time you and I met, and our child was born. I almost keep forgetting what we call her. Is it Sofi or Sofia? Or is that sophistry.' And Jenny said, 'What is not.'

Jenny had a family that had adopted her in Ireland. She said, ‘But they’ve sorted out that one quite nicely. What is happening now is the possibility of understanding what is happening, not by the use of words, whose job it is to always be pointing out—look, it’s either one thing or the other – but rather how to coordinate one’s own ability to be part of it. People in Ireland usually seem to manage this better than others.’

They first went to stay in the flat where Cyril lived when he was at home, and not travelling around the world trying to put coordination, like a dance, on film. He had said that he would not be coming home for a month or two and would very much welcome their staying in his flat when he was not there. Richard had been doing some work for his father, Mark, who had intimated too that he would be very pleased if they would look after his property while he was away. Mark/Cyril? had also said, if there was time, ‘l would be glad if you came across any read that you think would work for me – that is all this stuff that cannot be researched but can be looked at, around, or into with the hope not so much as to explain something but rather as to get somewhere.' Jenny had said, 'What I'd like to do is to go to Dover and then hop over to Calais.' Cyril had said, 'And you were once a refugee yourself.' Jenny had said, 'I was never a refugee. I was born in a strange country.' Cyril had said, 'To understand it. And what about Sophocles, or whatever you now call him.' Jenny said, 'What do you expect. He'll come along too.' Richard said, 'If she wants to.' As things worked out, the child went to stay for a time with Jenny's relations in Ireland while Jenny and Richard made plans for their trip to Calais.

What was at the heart of their interest, and also that of Cyril, which Richard wanted to write about and Cyril wanted to make a documentary film about, was the extraordinary state of affairs in both Europe and the Middle East, in which stories of violence, warfare, suffering, and hunger were mixed altogether in a way that seemed to work with the so-called refugees being able to get through in considerable numbers to the countries they hoped to go to. And even more extraordinarily, these countries were happy to accept them. This was what Cyril said he was trying to find out more about. He had got as far as explaining that many of the world's large-scale problems, which were in almost everyone's interests to solve, were brought to nothing by the strange obsession of humans that all this had to be explicable and validated by words – presumably because otherwise those in power might be cruelly held to account, even by those who agreed with them. Cyril and Richard, when they had had their talks together on the coast of the Mediterranean Sea, had seemed to be in communal states of mind, putting reason or loyalty to old stories above inquiry and understanding of how affairs in the world worked within the interplay of humans. When they reached England, both Richard and Cyril got copies of Jaspers's essays on the nineteenth century because they had dim memories of how Jaspers had foretold this situation of warfare and sterility might be glimpsed changing in the early twenty-first century. Richard would say, 'Can't you just put it that people got fed up with war.' Cyril said, 'I don't see evidence for that. It is more that they can't make up stories anymore that have any connection with reason or satisfaction.'

Richard said, 'And thank god Christians and Moslems seemed to have looked clearly at the evidence themselves. All but a few Moslems, that is, who get satisfaction from shooting people indiscriminately or chopping off their heads.' Cyril said, 'You mean, like Richard and Henry the Eighth did.' Jenny said, 'And yet most people don't seem to notice this. And then how does one change one's mind-set by efforts of one's own mind.' Cyril said, 'Yes, you mean without the help of people like Mohammed or Plato.' Richard said, 'People don't even find it easy to make the connections between the way there is now talk about jungle. One can presumably say that in the pre-Moses pre-Plato age humans with their mind and senses must have had an affinity with animals living in jungles. There were habits, instincts in them, which they would just have recognised, like watching evolution take its course.' Cyril said, 'And even then, only changing under the spell of hypnotic dramatists and profits.' And so now Jenny said, 'That is why Richard and I can say that we are so keen to go and have a look at what humans now call their own Jungle.' Someone who was sitting next to them in the cafe where they were talking said, 'Why?' Jenny replied, 'Because then perhaps we can go back there, all these thousands of years, and find we have learnt to emerge in a different way.' The people at the next table looked like students. Cyril said, half turned towards the students, 'And that's how one can learn and perhaps change.' One of the students said, 'Have you got children?' Richard said, 'Yes, you can do it with them.' Jenny said, 'It's more like, thank god, they can do it with us.' Cyril said, 'Their child is with its mother's relations in Ireland.' Richard said, 'Where quite a lot has changed.' One of the students said, 'Without planning? With just "give it a go"? "Guts." "Love".' Cyril said, 'Those are the passwords.'

*

The camp for refugees from the East that had grown up outside the French channel port of Calais was known as The Jungle. People who went there to see for themselves were either rather sardonic or were apt to find themselves going off on a parallel expedition in their mind. This journey around the outskirts of the Jungle went in a little and came out wondering, well that is not what I would have called a jungle. Then, of course, I have never really been in one; except maybe as a tourist in a Land Rover. And then I must say I do remember what seemed to be the extraordinary orderliness of jungle life; huge birds at the top of enormously tall trees, halfway down, lemurs and monkeys, smaller and then larger as one reaches the ground. At ground level everything seemed to be making its own way, finding its own home, not interfering with other species unless – I don't know what. Both the fierce animals and the huge animals seem to find more room for themselves on the planes and so 'jungle' seems to describe a state of natural orderliness which is helped by the extent of undergrowth providing natural shelter. Richard's description of the so-called 'Jungle' outside Calais, where refugees from Africa, as well as from Afghanistan and the Middle East, many of them having carried equipment and materials to make shelters for themselves when the possibility for this occurred, had set to achieving this orderliness, paying their respect to others doing the same with minimal intrusion. The Calais Jungle had no sense, of course, of the overwhelming dominance of nature, but rather with a striking sense of the rectitude of human instinct, if it was given a chance. That is, there were innumerable small tents and huts made from packing cases, or of wood; whatever waste matter might have been picked up on the way. The walls were either of material, or were intruding on each other physically, but it did appear, Richard insisted, to be in the natural order of events. The contact that humans had with one another, of all families, was a matter that existed, once accepted, without the necessity of further effort, least of all speech. Humans were there like the flowers or shrubs in a garden and only a quick nod of recognition was necessary if things went wrong. The beings who attracted most attention to themselves, even if still silently, seemed to be children; they would give notice that they liked being recognised and appreciated if that was all. At this first and indeed only visit to the Calais Jungle, Richard and Jenny spent a few days learning as much as they could, if their reaction were what they called real. In one sense they did not make any further friends, in another sense they became friends with the whole encampment.

*

In the evening of their first day's visit to the camp outside Calais, Richard and Jenny and the child, who was now called Sophie, were walking back along a road which seemed to epitomise a traffic jam. Sophie or Sophocles as he was sometimes known said, 'But then, if it suits them, why can't they stay there forever?' That's the sort of question which does not contain its answer. They were walking, as they so usually did, side by side with Sophie in the middle. Sophie said, 'People so often want to be alone and when they are, they want to be together, and so on and so on.' Richard said, 'So if that works, why do anything about it.' Sophie said, 'But it doesn't. Unless they never really want to get what they want.' Jenny said, 'Well, they never really do, do they.' Richard said, 'They've got it wrong about sex.' Sophie said, 'What about sex?' 'When you're getting it, it brings its own troubles.' Sophie said, 'l don't know about sex.' Jenny said, 'You're so lucky.' Sophie said, 'But I will do, won't I.' Richard said, 'Yes.'

They walked on. In the packed cars and vans at the edges, and just off the road, there were people, often families, sitting with just their faces visible staring out of windows. Jenny said, 'Sex was useful for animals, without it they would not have children.' Sophie said, 'Why did they want children?' Richard said, 'Because they wanted to have sex.' Sophie said, 'So there was a muzzle.' The child said, 'Sex was a bad thing because it caused trouble, but it was a good thing because it produced children.' Richard said, 'That's right.' The child said, 'And the result is more and more people are sitting in bands not moving, but they are looking out of windows.' Richard said, 'And it's a bad thing to talk too much about it.' Sophie said, 'Why?' Jenny said, 'Because then you seem to want it.' The child said, 'Otherwise the human race would die.' Jenny said, 'Which, for a time, seemed more and more likely.' The child said, 'Why?' Richard said, 'What's wrong with looking out of windows.' The child said, 'Then you don't have children.' Richard said,

'The way we got you was that we went hand in hand, into the wood.' Jenny said, 'We wanted to change the world. And we got you.' They walked on. After a silence, the child said, 'Then I wanted to jump off a cliff.' Richard said, 'Yes, why did you?' The child said, 'To do something for those people looking out of windows.' Richard said, 'What's wrong with looking out of windows?' Jenny said, 'That's all we do, anyway.' The child said, 'You mean, our eyes are windows.' Richard said, 'Or mirrors.' The child said, 'I don't even know what I look like.' Jenny said, 'No. Other people do.'

As they were walking along between the two rows of jammed cars, tractors, and lorries, they came to a camper van, or sort of minibus, which had a row of three windows behind the driver's compartment. At the windows, inside the van, there were three faces pressed close against them, looking out across the road on which Richard and Jenny and the child were walking. Richard thought – But I have seen those faces – that face – before, at the entrance or exit to the Holocaust Museum outside Jerusalem, where I had gone on my own, or was it with my father, Mark. I had thought then – how are they to be rescued.

In the space between the two jammed lines of cars outside Calais, Richard and Jenny and the child had stopped. The child had gone up to the minibus or camper van and was looking up at the faces of the three children pressed against the glass. The three faces looked down at him and seemed to be in some sort of communication with him. Richard and Jenny had stopped in the road and were watching the scene. Richard said, 'What are they saying?' Jenny said, 'I don't understand the language.' Richard said, 'What do you, did you, understand?' Jenny said, 'I was picked up and taken away.' Richard said, 'Who by?' Jenny said, 'That Joanna, who may or may not be your mother.'

The man and the woman in the driving compartment of the van had turned and were looking at Richard and Jenny. Richard walked briskly to the driver's seat door and pulled it open. He said, 'All right, get out.' The man behind the driving wheel turned to the woman sitting beside him and without hesitation the woman said, 'All right, get out.' Jenny had gone to the back of the van and opened the door there: the three children who had been inside were climbing out. Richard said to the man who had been driving, 'Have you got a gun.' The man said, 'Yes.' The woman went back to the van and, from a space behind the driving seat, lifted out two old-fashioned rifles. She carried these back to where Richard and the child and three somewhat older children were standing. She handed the guns one to Richard and one to Jenny. Jenny said, 'No you keep them.' The woman handed them to the man from the van who had been beside her. The woman said to Jenny, 'We want to get to England.' Richard said, 'You are under some sort of apprehension.' Richard was thinking – so it wasn't misapprehension all those years ago, but recognition had to be confirmed by the child. The child, who had so far not spoken during this encounter, said, as if to Jenny, 'Will they get to where they want to go?' Jenny said, 'I suppose so, if all goes well.' Richard said, 'Now walk ahead of us; as if you are under enforcement.' The man who had been driver of the van said, 'But we are not.' The woman who had been with them said, 'Well it certainly looks like it.'

The seven of them began walking up the road to where the traffic jam ended and the camp began. Jenny said, as if to Richard, over the head of the child, 'There's the guardhouse ahead. They will sort things out.' Richard said, 'We will say we know them and we'll vouch for them.' The child began to run, and skip, slightly ahead of them, doing a strange dance of his own invention. At the barrier across the road there were armed soldiers in both French and English uniforms watching the child. Jenny went ahead and spoke to whoever was behind the open hatch of the guardhouse. One of the guards began half-heartedly, then with increased vigour, to emulate, or as if in partnership with the child in his dance, to lift the barrier. The child ducked under it and went through; and the guards lifted the barrier so that the others could follow.

POSTSCRIPT
Saving Humanity, or How to Enter a Partnership with God

'I would believe only in a god that knows how to dance'

'Man is a rope stretched between the animal and the Superman – a rope over an abyss . . . a bridge and not a goal'

Friedrich Nietzsche,
Thus Spake Zarathustra

I met Nicholas Mosley for the first time in London in 1994. I was an English literature student who had come all the way from Germany in search of firsthand material for a thesis on the novels of Nicholas Mosley. I had come across his work through the recommendation of my former literature teacher at school and felt I had never read anything quite like *Hopeful Monsters* (which won the Whitbread Book of the Year Award in 1990). Set in England and Germany in the interwar years – the 1920s – it carries the reader through the troubled history of Europe and the entire world, into the 20th century and the New World Order.

I was struck by the love story. It made me feel liberated in the sense that it enabled me to see the bigger picture. Of course, I'd already heard and read a lot about love being a liberating and empowering force. Most love stories I'd read till then, however – when they didn't end in tragedy – offered unconvincing and cliché happy endings. And even if the happy ending was convincing, the reader couldn't imagine what the couple would go on to do once their passion had been sated. In Jane Austen's *Pride and Prejudice*, Elizabeth's free spirit and independence were liberating. But what do you do with yourself as Mrs Darcy? Where was the bigger picture? Where was the higher plane to which her love was supposed to carry her? In contrast, in *Hopeful Monsters*, the love and life of Eleanor Anders, the young German-Jewish scientist whose relationship with the Englishman Max Ackerman spans six decades, was liberating to read. Through her enduring – but unorthodox – love for Max, she not only led a fulfilling life as a woman and a scientist, travelling half the world, but could also envision a new type of human being that could save the world and humanity from extinction.

My fascination with *Hopeful Monsters* quickly gave way to surprise when I found out that very little had been published in academic research on Mosley and his writings. I needed secondary sources in order to embark on my thesis, so I wrote a letter to Mosley's publisher Secker and Warburg, explaining what I was looking for and was pleasantly surprised (I thought my letter would end up in a bin or under a huge pile of unanswered letters) when Nicholas Mosley wrote back to me himself, and gave me a date and a time at which I could visit him at his large Victorian house on a quiet, leafy crescent just a stone's throw from the buzz of Camden Town.

Once I was in front of him – a very charming, very tall, very English man with large hands and lively eyes looking at me from behind black-framed glasses – he warned me about his stammer (which varied in intensity) and then sank into an old armchair in the reception room of his basement flat. He joked about his study, which was in the basement, as the seat of the subconscious: his wife, a psychotherapist, had the rest of the four floors of the large house all to herself. He seemed quite pleased that I wasn't there because of his father, Oswald Mosley, who had founded the British Union of Fascists in the 1930s (the English fascist movement of the 1930s isn't deemed important in Germany, where I'd spent most of my youth), but only because I was interested in his novels of ideas. He had just finished his autobiography *Efforts at Truth*, and he informed me that the autobiography was to be the seal to his artistic career. He was mistaken. The following twenty years proved to be one of the most productive phases of his life: he published around a dozen books and various articles in that period.

Love was what we mainly talked about for the next twenty-five years. For Mosley, love is a framework or a safety net, where lovers can experiment with ways and possibilities of being in partnership with a greater force – history, evolution, God, an all-encompassing consciousness. Within this framework, they can influence the course of humanity and save it from 'a dangerous across, a dangerous on-the-way, a dangerous looking-back, a dangerous shuddering and stopping.'[1]. For the lovers in *Hopeful Monsters*, the threat of humanity's extinction becomes reality when the atomic bomb – in whose development Max the physicist actually takes part, only to protest against its use in the anti-nuclear Aldermaston protests – is tested by the Americans in Japan, killing hundreds of thousands.

So, what experiments can save humanity? Can humans learn from their mistakes, and evolve into higher beings that can 'become a rope over the Abyss [. . .] a bridge and not a goal' and thus save themselves from extinction? This question has been at the heart of Nicholas Mosley's literary experiment for the past twenty-five years.

In the introduction to his last novel, *Rainbow People*, Mosley refers to one of his favourite (apart from Nietzsche) German philosophers, Karl Jaspers. Jaspers noted a major shift in

1 Friedrich Nietzsche, *Thus Spoke Zarathustra,* (London: Random House, 1995), p. 14.

human consciousness, beginning nearly three millennia ago. At this time, when religions emerged, Jaspers remarked, human beings stopped being led wholly by their instincts. Now gods started speaking to humans through prophets, or rather poet-prophets, and showing them the way. All humans had to do was obey. This worked well until the Greeks entered the scene. The Greek dramatists, philosophers, scientists and mathematicians showed that humans were not limited to obeying an instinct or the words of gods in order to survive: they could survive by doing the job of gods; in other words, by developing a will to face their predicaments. So Jasper sees the age of the Greeks – around 500 BCE – as the age when human beings learned to be conscious of their animal instincts. Their awareness of this ability made them feel like supernatural beings that had come from heaven! At the same time, the Greek philosophers, scientists and dramatists showed that humans had the talent to express this consciousness in their own way, by means of art, drama, music and mathematics. Whereas the Old Testament God spoke from the heavens to more or less will-less humans, the Greeks seemed to be saying that humans could work out their dilemmas through their own effort, by registering what they observed and enacting it on stage or in poetry or in mathematical formulae or in music. In all these ways, humans could understand what it was that the gods wanted from them.

In Mosley's understanding of Jaspers, the next stage in the evolution of human consciousness begins at the beginning of the third millennium – around 2000 CE. That was the dawn of the era when humans discovered that they not only have a talent to understand what God means, but may one day have the talent to represent that meaning. For Mosley, this is where love comes in. Love is a framework – or space – where man and God can negotiate as equals and thus become partners in creation. Dance, for Mosley, is the most fitting metaphor for this partnership. When two people are dancing, they must trust each other in order to be able to follow each other's steps and weave a pattern, a choreography. If they don't, they'll end up stepping on each other's feet and dancing will become impossible. In order to trust God, people must realise that their role is not one of obedience or disobedience, but that of one half of a partnership where harmony and art and beauty can evolve. Great scientists, mathematicians and philosophers, from Plato and Pythagoras to Galileo and Leibniz, saw the direct relationship between art (i.e. beauty) and science. It was seeing this correlation that allowed humankind to participate in creation – in the dance of creation – and become God's partner in saving humanity.

In *Hopeful Monsters*, Mosley investigates this idea from a historical point of view. *Hopeful Monsters* is at once a historical novel and a novel of ideas about two young scientists, Eleanor and Max, growing up in the turbulent Twenties and Thirties in Europe, where old orders and old systems of thought, society and science were cracking up. In his portrait of the love of the two protagonists, Mosley looks at the condition of humankind in the twentieth century and the evolution of a 'new human type' in what Nietzsche called 'the great hundred-act play reserved for the next two centuries in Europe; the most terrible, the most questionable, the most hopeful of all plays'.[2]

The phrase 'hopeful monsters' is itself borrowed from the German-American biologist Goldschmidt, who used it to describe the appearance of new species through mutations in a relatively short period of time. Goldschmidt's theory of evolution, as opposed to Darwinian gradualism, postulated an evolutionary process that took place in big jumps.[3] Mosley appropriated this idea in order to define his protagonists as 'mutants' – as the new, hopefully viable

---

2 Friedrich Nietzsche, *On the Genealogy of Morality*, (Cambridge: Cambridge University Press, 2006), p. 119.

3 Richard B. Goldschmidt, *The Material Basis of Evolution*, (New Haven & London: Yale University Press, 1982), p. 390.

strand who represent a future possibility for the evolution of their old and threatened species.

After meeting the Lamarckian biologist, Dr Kammerer, the young Max embarks on an experiment with salamanders in hope of discovering an alternative to Darwinian biology. (The Lamarckians believed that it was possible for acquired characteristics that have proved advantageous for the parent generation to be genetically passed on to their offspring.) Max tries to prove this theory by changing the environment of a pair of lowland salamanders, whose offspring are usually born in water, and getting them to reproduce in the manner of the alpine salamanders; that is, by giving birth not to larvae but to fully formed offspring. He wants to see whether an organism's ability to observe itself in a given situation and *learn* to do away with patterns that were once useful, but in a new environment prove deleterious, can help it 'pull out' the 'right' mutation from the multitude of mutations to which it has access, in order to adapt itself to its new environment.

The fact that he calls his salamanders 'hopeful monsters' is all too appropriate.

In this experiment, Max does not 'isolate' certain mutations to propagate them, but prepares the ground that will allow the seeds of specific mutations to grow. The seeds – or mutations – are there. They float or fly and fall and settle when they have reached the right environment. Hopeful monsters create an environment in which the right seeds may fall and grow.

For Mosley, as for the Greeks, creation is beauty. And beauty is only possible where there is love. Max lovingly creates beautiful surroundings for his 'hopeful monsters' so that they can have their offspring. The survival of the salamander's offspring can be read as a harbinger of the emergence of a new type of human being that might save humanity from annihilating itself.

The survival of this new creature is the main topic of the novel *Rainbow People*, the third and last book in the thought-experiment that became Mosley's *Metamorphosis Trilogy*. The title *Rainbow People* alludes to the term 'rainbow children', which, as Mosley explains in the introduction, is used by educationalists to refer to the emergence of children 'different enough to make them distinct from normality by virtue of the intensity of their curiosity for how things worked [...] combined with a gentleness and even sweetness of disposition to others'.[4] In this novel, Mosley depicts the current refugee crisis as a possible catalyst for the evolution of rainbow people – the saviours of humanity. In his eyes, a rainbow is something that not only aesthetically resembles a bridge between two worlds, but is also the aesthetic embodiment of a scientific process involving two different forms of existence: energy (i.e. sunlight) and matter (i.e. drops of water). The rainbow is the aesthetic embodiment of a collision. It symbolizes an opportunity to turn things into beauty, to bridge and cross frontiers – God willing.

This is the crux of Mosley's novel. God can

4 Introduction to *Rainbow People*, (London: Dalkey Archive Press, 2017).

only will something if humankind enters into partnership with Him and becomes His equal, like Nietzsche's dancers. The refugee child at the end of the novel does this through a little dance. When I asked why the child at the end of the novel must dance around the frontier guard in order to get to the other side, Mosley winked: 'Silly fool! You can't put your feet on a rainbow bridge! You could only cross a bridge made of sunlight and raindrops without falling if you danced on it!' The frontier guard would only lift the barrier if there was some partnership between him and the refugee child. A dance is a perfect way to express this trust.[5]

Shiva Rahbaran, London, Winter of 2017

---

5 For more on Mosley and his oeuvre see my book *The Paradox of Freedom: A Study of the Life and Writings of Nicholas Mosley* (London: Dalkey Archive Press, 2007).

Jungle Camp, Calais, France, April 2016
© Shiva Rahbaran

Nicholas Mosley (1923-2017) was born in London and was educated at Eton and Oxford. He served in Italy during World War II, and published his first novel, *Spaces of the Dark*, in 1951. During his career, he published more than 20 novels and books of nonfiction, including *Accident* and *Impossible Object,* which were both turned into films, and *Hopeful Monsters*, which won the 1990 Whitbread Book of the Year Award. His most notable works of nonfiction include the autobiography *Efforts at Truth,* and a two-part biography of his father, Sir Oswald Mosley, entitled *Rules of the Game* and *Beyond the Pale*.

SELECTED DALKEY ARCHIVE TITLES

MICHAL AJVAZ, *The Golden Age.*
The Other City.

PIERRE ALBERT-BIROT, *Grabinoulor.*

YUZ ALESHKOVSKY, *Kangaroo.*

SVETLANA ALEXIEVICH, *Voices from Chernobyl.*

FELIPE ALFAU, *Chromos.*
Locos.

JOAO ALMINO, *Enigmas of Spring.*

IVAN ÂNGELO, *The Celebration.*
The Tower of Glass.

ANTÓNIO LOBO ANTUNES, *Knowledge of Hell.*
The Splendor of Portugal.

ALAIN ARIAS-MISSON, *Theatre of Incest.*

JOHN ASHBERY & JAMES SCHUYLER, *A Nest of Ninnies.*

GABRIELA AVIGUR-ROTEM, *Heatwave and Crazy Birds.*

DJUNA BARNES, *Ladies Almanack.*
Ryder.

JOHN BARTH, *Letters.*
Sabbatical.
Collected Stories.

DONALD BARTHELME, *The King.*
Paradise.

SVETISLAV BASARA, *Chinese Letter.*
Fata Morgana.
In Search of the Grail.

MIQUEL BAUÇÀ, *The Siege in the Room.*

RENÉ BELLETTO, *Dying.*

MAREK BIENCZYK, *Transparency.*

ANDREI BITOV, *Pushkin House.*

ANDREJ BLATNIK, *You Do Understand.*
Law of Desire.

LOUIS PAUL BOON, *Chapel Road.*
My Little War.
Summer in Termuren.

ROGER BOYLAN, *Killoyle.*

IGNÁCIO DE LOYOLA BRANDÃO, *Anonymous Celebrity.*
Zero.

BRIGID BROPHY, *In Transit.*
The Prancing Novelist.

GABRIELLE BURTON, *Heartbreak Hotel.*

MICHEL BUTOR, *Degrees.*
Mobile.

G. CABRERA INFANTE, *Infante's Inferno.*
Three Trapped Tigers.

JULIETA CAMPOS, *The Fear of Losing Eurydice.*

ANNE CARSON, *Eros the Bittersweet.*

ORLY CASTEL-BLOOM, *Dolly City.*

LOUIS-FERDINAND CÉLINE, *North.*
Conversations with Professor Y.
London Bridge.

HUGO CHARTERIS, *The Tide Is Right.*

ERIC CHEVILLARD, *Demolishing Nisard.*
The Author and Me.

MARC CHOLODENKO, *Mordechai Schamz.*

EMILY HOLMES COLEMAN, *The Shutter of Snow.*

ERIC CHEVILLARD, *The Author and Me.*

LUIS CHITARRONI, *The No Variations.*

CH'OE YUN, *Mannequin.*

ROBERT COOVER, *A Night at the Movies.*

STANLEY CRAWFORD, *Log of the S.S. The Mrs Unguentine.*
Some Instructions to My Wife.

RALPH CUSACK, *Cadenza.*

NICHOLAS DELBANCO, *Sherbrookes.*
The Count of Concord.

NIGEL DENNIS, *Cards of Identity.*

PETER DIMOCK, *A Short Rhetoric for Leaving the Family.*

ARIEL DORFMAN, *Konfidenz.*

COLEMAN DOWELL, *Island People.*
Too Much Flesh and Jabez.

RIKKI DUCORNET, *Phosphor in Dreamland.*
The Complete Butcher's Tales.

RIKKI DUCORNET (cont.), *The Jade Cabinet.*
The Fountains of Neptune.

WILLIAM EASTLAKE, *Castle Keep.*
Lyric of the Circle Heart.

JEAN ECHENOZ, *Chopin's Move.*

SELECTED DALKEY ARCHIVE TITLES

STANLEY ELKIN, *A Bad Man.*
The Dick Gibson Show.
The Franchiser.

FRANÇOIS EMMANUEL, *Invitation to a Voyage.*

SALVADOR ESPRIU, *Ariadne in the Grotesque Labyrinth.*

LESLIE A. FIEDLER, *Love and Death in the American Novel.*

JUAN FILLOY, *Op Oloop.*

GUSTAVE FLAUBERT, *Bouvard and Pécuchet.*

JON FOSSE, *Aliss at the Fire.*
Melancholy.
Trilogy.

FORD MADOX FORD, *The March of Literature.*

MAX FRISCH, *I'm Not Stiller.*
Man in the Holocene.

CARLOS FUENTES, *Christopher Unborn.*
Distant Relations.
Terra Nostra.
Where the Air Is Clear.
Nietzsche on His Balcony.

WILLIAM GADDIS, JR., *The Recognitions.*
JR.

JANICE GALLOWAY, *Foreign Parts.*
The Trick Is to Keep Breathing.

WILLIAM H. GASS, *Life Sentences.*
The Tunnel.
The World Within the Word.
Willie Masters' Lonesome Wife.

GÉRARD GAVARRY, *Hoppla! 1 2 3.*

ETIENNE GILSON, *The Arts of the Beautiful.*
Forms and Substances in the Arts.

C. S. GISCOMBE, *Giscome Road.*
Here.

DOUGLAS GLOVER, *Bad News of the Heart.*

WITOLD GOMBROWICZ, *A Kind of Testament.*

PAULO EMÍLIO SALES GOMES, *P's Three Women.*

GEORGI GOSPODINOV, *Natural Novel.*

JUAN GOYTISOLO, *Juan the Landless.*
Makbara.
Marks of Identity.

JACK GREEN, *Fire the Bastards!*

JIŘÍ GRUŠA, *The Questionnaire.*

MELA HARTWIG, *Am I a Redundant Human Being?*

JOHN HAWKES, *The Passion Artist.*
Whistlejacket.

ELIZABETH HEIGHWAY, ED., *Contemporary Georgian Fiction.*

AIDAN HIGGINS, *Balcony of Europe.*
Blind Man's Bluff.
Bornholm Night-Ferry.
Langrishe, Go Down.
Scenes from a Receding Past.

ALDOUS HUXLEY, *Antic Hay.*
Point Counter Point.
Those Barren Leaves.
Time Must Have a Stop.

JANG JUNG-IL, *When Adam Opens His Eyes*

DRAGO JANČAR, *The Tree with No Name.*
I Saw Her That Night.
Galley Slave.

MIKHEIL JAVAKHISHVILI, *Kvachi.*

GERT JONKE, *The Distant Sound.*
Homage to Czerny.
The System of Vienna.

JACQUES JOUET, *Mountain R.*
Savage.
Upstaged.

JUNG YOUNG-MOON, *A Contrived World.*

MIEKO KANAI, *The Word Book.*

YORAM KANIUK, *Life on Sandpaper.*

ZURAB KARUMIDZE, *Dagny.*

PABLO KATCHADJIAN, *What to Do.*

JOHN KELLY, *From Out of the City.*

HUGH KENNER, *Flaubert, Joyce and Beckett: The Stoic Comedians.*
Joyce's Voices.

DANILO KIŠ, *The Attic.*
The Lute and the Scars.
Psalm 44.
A Tomb for Boris Davidovich.

ANITA KONKKA, *A Fool's Paradise.*

GEORGE KONRÁD, *The City Builder.*
TADEUSZ KONWICKI, *A Minor Apocalypse.*
The Polish Complex.
ELAINE KRAF, *The Princess of 72nd Street.*
JIM KRUSOE, *Iceland.*
AYSE KULIN, *Farewell: A Mansion in Occupied Istanbul.*
EMILIO LASCANO TEGUI, *On Elegance While Sleeping.*
ERIC LAURRENT, *Do Not Touch.*
VIOLETTE LEDUC, *La Bâtarde.*
LEE KI-HO, *At Least We Can Apologize.*
EDOUARD LEVÉ, *Autoportrait.*
Suicide.
MARIO LEVI, *Istanbul Was a Fairy Tale.*
DEBORAH LEVY, *Billy and Girl.*
JOSÉ LEZAMA LIMA, *Paradiso.*
OSMAN LINS, *Avalovara.*
The Queen of the Prisons of Greece.
ALF MACLOCHLAINN, *Out of Focus.*
Past Habitual.
RON LOEWINSOHN, *Magnetic Field(s).*
YURI LOTMAN, *Non-Memoirs.*
D. KEITH MANO, *Take Five.*
MINA LOY, *Stories and Essays of Mina Loy.*
MICHELINE AHARONIAN MARCOM, *The Mirror in the Well.*
BEN MARCUS, *The Age of Wire and String.*
WALLACE MARKFIELD, *Teitlebaum's Window.*
To an Early Grave.
DAVID MARKSON, *Reader's Block.*
Wittgenstein's Mistress.
CAROLE MASO, *AVA.*
HISAKI MATSUURA, *Triangle.*
LADISLAV MATEJKA & KRYSTYNA POMORSKA, EDS., *Readings in Russian Poetics: Formalist & Structuralist Views.*
HARRY MATHEWS, *Cigarettes.*
The Conversions.
The Human Country.
The Journalist.
My Life in CIA.
Singular Pleasures.
The Sinking of the Odradek.
Stadium.
Tlooth.
JOSEPH MCELROY, *Night Soul and Other Stories.*
ABDELWAHAB MEDDEB, *Talismano.*
GERHARD MEIER, *Isle of the Dead.*
HERMAN MELVILLE, *The Confidence-Man.*
AMANDA MICHALOPOULOU, *I'd Like.*
STEVEN MILLHAUSER, *The Barnum Museum.*
In the Penny Arcade.
RALPH J. MILLS, JR., *Essays on Poetry.*
CHRISTINE MONTALBETTI, *The Origin of Man.*
Western.
NICHOLAS MOSLEY, *Accident.*
Assassins.
Catastrophe Practice.
Hopeful Monsters.
Imago Bird.
Natalie Natalia.
Serpent.
WARREN MOTTE, *Fiction Now: The French Novel in the 21st Century.*
Oulipo: A Primer of Potential Literature.
GERALD MURNANE, *Barley Patch.*
Inland.
YVES NAVARRE, *Our Share of Time.*
Sweet Tooth.
DOROTHY NELSON, *In Night's City.*
Tar and Feathers.
WILFRIDO D. NOLLEDO, *But for the Lovers.*
BORIS A. NOVAK, *The Master of Insomnia.*
FLANN O'BRIEN, *At Swim-Two-Birds.*
The Best of Myles.
The Dalkey Archive.
The Hard Life.
The Poor Mouth.
The Third Policeman.
CLAUDE OLLIER, *The Mise-en-Scène.*
Wert and the Life Without End.

SELECTED DALKEY ARCHIVE TITLES

PATRIK OUŘEDNÍK, *Europeana.*
The Opportune Moment, 1855.

BORIS PAHOR, *Necropolis.*

FERNANDO DEL PASO, *News from the Empire.*
Palinuro of Mexico.

ROBERT PINGET, *The Inquisitory.*
Mahu or The Material.
Trio.

MANUEL PUIG, *Betrayed by Rita Hayworth.*
The Buenos Aires Affair.
Heartbreak Tango.

RAYMOND QUENEAU, *The Last Days.*
Odile.
Pierrot Mon Ami.
Saint Glinglin.

ANN QUIN, *Berg.*
Passages.
Three.
Tripticks.

ISHMAEL REED, *The Free-Lance Pallbearers.*
The Last Days of Louisiana Red.
Ishmael Reed: The Plays.
Juice!
The Terrible Threes.
The Terrible Twos.
Yellow Back Radio Broke-Down.

RAINER MARIA RILKE,
The Notebooks of Malte Laurids Brigge.

JULIÁN RÍOS, *The House of Ulysses.*
Larva: A Midsummer Night's Babel.
Poundemonium.

ALAIN ROBBE-GRILLET, *Project for a Revolution in New York.*
A Sentimental Novel.

AUGUSTO ROA BASTOS, *I the Supreme.*

DANIËL ROBBERECHTS, *Arriving in Avignon.*

JEAN ROLIN, *The Explosion of the Radiator Hose.*

OLIVIER ROLIN, *Hotel Crystal.*

ALIX CLEO ROUBAUD, *Alix's Journal.*

JACQUES ROUBAUD, *The Form of a City Changes Faster, Alas, Than the Human Heart.*
The Great Fire of London.
Hortense in Exile.
Hortense Is Abducted.
Mathematics: The Plurality of Worlds of Lewis.
Some Thing Black.

RAYMOND ROUSSEL, *Impressions of Africa.*

VEDRANA RUDAN, *Night.*

GERMAN SADULAEV, *The Maya Pill.*

TOMAŽ ŠALAMUN, *Soy Realidad.*

LYDIE SALVAYRE, *The Company of Ghosts.*

LUIS RAFAEL SÁNCHEZ, *Macho Camacho's Beat.*

SEVERO SARDUY, *Cobra & Maitreya.*

NATHALIE SARRAUTE, *Do You Hear Them?*
Martereau.
The Planetarium.

STIG SÆTERBAKKEN, *Siamese.*
Self-Control.
Through the Night.

ARNO SCHMIDT, *Collected Novellas.*
Collected Stories.
Nobodaddy's Children.
Two Novels.

ASAF SCHURR, *Motti.*

GAIL SCOTT, *My Paris.*

JUNE AKERS SEESE,
Is This What Other Women Feel Too?

BERNARD SHARE, *Inish.*
Transit.

VIKTOR SHKLOVSKY, *Bowstring.*
Literature and Cinematography.
Theory of Prose.
Third Factory.
Zoo, or Letters Not about Love.

PIERRE SINIAC, *The Collaborators.*

KJERSTI A. SKOMSVOLD,
The Faster I Walk, the Smaller I Am.

JOSEF ŠKVORECKÝ, *The Engineer of Human Souls.*

GILBERT SORRENTINO, *Aberration of Starlight.*
Blue Pastoral.
Crystal Vision.

FOR A FULL LIST OF PUBLICATIONS, VISIT: www.dalkeyarchive.com

SELECTED DALKEY ARCHIVE TITLES

Imaginative Qualities of Actual Things.
Mulligan Stew.
Red the Fiend.
Steelwork.
Under the Shadow.

ANDRZEJ STASIUK, *Dukla.*
Fado.

GERTRUDE STEIN, *The Making of Americans.*
A Novel of Thank You.

PIOTR SZEWC, *Annihilation.*

GONÇALO M. TAVARES, *A Man: Klaus Klump.*
Jerusalem.
Learning to Pray in the Age of Technique.

LUCIAN DAN TEODOROVICI, *Our Circus Presents . . .*

NIKANOR TERATOLOGEN, *Assisted Living.*

STEFAN THEMERSON, *Hobson's Island.*
The Mystery of the Sardine.
Tom Harris.

JOHN TOOMEY, *Sleepwalker.*
Huddleston Road.
Slipping.

DUMITRU TSEPENEAG, *Hotel Europa.*
The Necessary Marriage.
Pigeon Post.
Vain Art of the Fugue.
La Belle Roumaine.
Waiting: Stories.

ESTHER TUSQUETS, *Stranded.*

DUBRAVKA UGRESIC, *Lend Me Your Character.*
Thank You for Not Reading.

TOR ULVEN, *Replacement.*

MATI UNT, *Brecht at Night.*
Diary of a Blood Donor.
Things in the Night.

ÁLVARO URIBE & OLIVIA SEARS, EDS., *Best of Contemporary Mexican Fiction.*

ELOY URROZ, *Friction.*
The Obstacles.

LUISA VALENZUELA, *Dark Desires and the Others.*
He Who Searches.

PAUL VERHAEGHEN, *Omega Minor.*

BORIS VIAN, *Heartsnatcher.*

TOOMAS VINT, *An Unending Landscape.*

ORNELA VORPSI, *The Country Where No One Ever Dies.*

AUSTRYN WAINHOUSE, *Hedyphagetica.*

MARKUS WERNER, *Cold Shoulder.*
Zundel's Exit.

CURTIS WHITE, *The Idea of Home.*
Memories of My Father Watching TV.
Requiem.

DIANE WILLIAMS, *Excitability: Selected Stories.*

DOUGLAS WOOLF, *Wall to Wall.*
Ya! & John-Juan.

JAY WRIGHT, *Polynomials and Pollen.*
The Presentable Art of Reading Absence.

PHILIP WYLIE, *Generation of Vipers.*

MARGUERITE YOUNG, *Angel in the Forest.*
Miss MacIntosh, My Darling.

REYOUNG, *Unbabbling.*

ZORAN ŽIVKOVIĆ , *Hidden Camera.*

LOUIS ZUKOFSKY, *Collected Fiction.*

VITOMIL ZUPAN, *Minuet for Guitar.*

SCOTT ZWIREN, *God Head.*

AND MORE . . .